A note from the author

When the Covid-19 lockdown hit, like so many others, I found my world turned upside down. I had been making my living as a freelance filmmaker, but under quarantine, the work disappeared entirely. Financially unstable, I moved back to my dad's house. Schools were closed and my seven-year-old brother and sister, Cai and Sora, were now learning at home. With my dad, a professor of epidemiology, called back to work for the NHS, I found myself spending more time than ever before being a big brother, a cook, a teacher, and a human climbing frame.

Writing *The Great Realisation* was a challenge I set myself: if there was a hopeful message to be found, then I believed it should be. I can't pretend to have had an unbearable lockdown. Many people have faced much greater financial hardships or suffered the loneliness of isolation. There are families with children who have no gardens to play in, and parents who don't have the time or resources to home-school them. Millions of people around the world are grieving the loss of a loved one. *The Great Realisation* does not seek to negate the suffering of so many. All I want is to offer up a message of hope and optimism.

The Great Realisation is a bedtime story for a time of change. It is a reminder that we need not aim for a return just to normal when there is a tangible prospect of progress and the potential for so much more. It is the simple message of hope I found when I went looking.

I hope you find some use in this story, and that you find and share your own.

Tom

For Cai and Sora – T.R.

For my nieces and nephews – N.

First published in Great Britain 2020 by Egmont Books UK Ltd
2 Minster Court, London EC3R 7BB | www.egmontbooks.co.uk
Text and illustrations © Probably Tomfoolery Limited 2020 | Illustrations by Nomoco
The moral rights of Tomos Roberts have been asserted.
ISBN 978 0 7555 0150 2 | 71467/001 | Printed in Italy.
A CIP catalogue record for this book is available from the British Library.

THE GREAT REALISATION

Tomos Roberts

With art by Nomoco

EGMONT

*"Tell me the one about the virus again,
  then I'll go to bed."*

But, my boy, you're growing weary,
sleepy thoughts about your head.

*"**Please!** That one's my favourite.
I promise, just once more –
Take me back to 2020.
That's all I'm asking for."*

Okay, snuggle down,
my boy, though I know
you know full well,
the story starts before then,
in a world I once
would dwell . . .

It was a world
of waste
and wonder,
of poverty
and plenty.

Back before
we understood
why hindsight's
2020.

You see, the people came up with companies,
to trade across all lands.

But they swelled and got much **bigger**
than we ever could have planned.

We'd always had our wants,
but now it got so quick.

You could have
anything you
dreamed of,

in a day
and with a

click.

We noticed families had stopped talking.
That's not to say they never spoke.

But the meaning must have melted
and the work—life balance broke.

And the children's
eyes grew squarer,
and every toddler
had a phone.

They filtered out
the imperfections,

but amidst the noise

they felt

alone.

Every day the skies grew thicker,
till you couldn't see the stars.

So we flew in planes to find them,

while down below
we filled our cars.

We'd drive around all day in circles.
We'd forgotten how to run.
We swapped the grass for tarmac,
shrunk the parks till there were none.

We filled the sea
with plastic,
'cause our waste
was never capped.

Until each day
when you went fishing,
you'd pull them out,
already wrapped.

And while we drank
    and smoked and gambled,
        our leaders taught us why
    it's best to not
    upset the lobbies –
        more convenient to die.

But then in 2020,

a new virus

came our way.

The governments

reacted,

told us all

to hide

away.

But while we all were hidden,
amidst the fear, and all the while . . .

We dusted off our instincts.

We remembered how to smile.

We started clapping to say thank you

and calling up our mums.

And while the car keys gathered dust,

we would look forward to our runs.

And with the skies less full of voyagers, the Earth began to breathe.

And the beaches bore new wildlife that scuttled off into the seas.

Some people started dancing,
some were singing,
some were baking.

We'd grown so used
to bad news,
but there was good news
in the making.

Old habits became extinct
and they made way

for the new.

And every
simple act of kindness
was now given its due.

And so when we found the cure, and were allowed to go outside . . .

We all preferred the world we found, to the one we'd left behind.

"But why did it take a virus
to bring the people back together?"

Well, sometimes you get sick, my boy,
    before you start
        feeling better.

So lie down and dream of tomorrow,
    and all the things that we can do.
        And who knows, if you dream hard enough,
            maybe some of them will come true.

We now call it
The Great Realisation
and, yes, since then
there have been many.

But that's the story
of how it started

and why
hindsight's
2020.